"What about me?"

asked T.J. He was getting really sick of being left out of the search for the pizza pie spies. "And don't tell me I'm in charge of headquarters."

"You're not headquarters anymore," Jimmy told him. "You're the eyes of the operation. Keeping careful watch through your telescope, never resting at your post, you survey the neighborhood. Nothing escapes your keen sight, heightened by a high-tech telescope. And even in the darkest shadows—"

Dottie interrupted with a loud sigh. "Just keep looking out the window, T.J., and see if anything strange turns up."

"Okay," T.J. agreed. He suddenly felt very tired. Dragging his blanket behind him like a long cape, he got off the couch and hobbled toward the stairs. "Tomorrow is going to be a long day. This private eye has to search for a spy."

THE CASE OF
The Pizza Pie
— Spy —

•

William Alexander

•

Troll Associates

Cover art: Judith Sutton
Illustrated by: Dave Henderson

Library of Congress Cataloging-in-Publication Data

Alexander, William, (date)
    The case of the pizza pie spy / by William Alexander.
        p.   cm.—(The Clues kids; #4)
    Summary: While searching for a bike thief, the Clues Kids, five
foster children living with Chief Klink and his wife, investigate
the suspicious activities at a local pizza parlor.
    ISBN 0-8167-1698-6 (lib. bdg.)   ISBN 0-8167-1699-4 (pbk.)
    [1. Mystery and detective stories. 2. Foster home care—Fiction.]
I. Title. II. Series: Alexander, William, 1950-   The Clues kids; #4.
PZ7.A3786Caw 1990
[Fic]—dc20   89-20156

A TROLL BOOK, published by Troll Associates,
Mahwah, NJ 07430

JAY LOCKE

Code name: Clicker—Jay takes the pictures...lots of pictures. No clue escapes his lens because he shoots everything—windows, pets, doorknobs, lint—everything.

T.J. BOOKER

Code name: Smoke Screen—T.J. is the greatest disguise artist in the world (he asked me to say that). Actually, he *does* make up some great disguises. Some of them are pretty strange...but that's T.J.

JIMMY LOCKE

Code name: Jaws—He's the information man. He asks the questions. With his razor-sharp mind (he *made* me say that), Jimmy can break down any suspect.

DOTTIE BREWSTER

Code name: Short Stuff—She's the normal one of the bunch. Dottie looks for clues, tails crooks, keeps track of their fees, and tries to keep the others out of trouble. That's harder than you think!

LEE VAN THO

Code name: Smudge—Lee gets the fingerprints. He really gets the fingerprints. He usually makes a mess getting the prints, but he gets them!

C·H·A·P·T·E·R
1

*D*ozerville, Illinois. Population 12,534. It used to be 12,533 and a half. But the half citizen, Boswell the chimp, was finally granted full status. That's just the kind of generous spirit folks in Dozerville are known for.

It's a peaceful little town like any other—well, maybe a little different. For one thing, it has twenty-six pizza parlors. The people of Dozerville admit that's a bit unusual, but they don't care. They love pizza.

Besides Boswell and lots of pizza parlors, Dozerville has something else that no other community can claim: the Clues Kids. A reporter once called them, "Five candy-bar-toting, bike-riding junior detectives ever on the lookout for villains and evildoers who dare to do their dastardly deeds in Dozerville." The reporter was out of breath after she said that.

Some consider the Clues Kids detectives. Others think they're a big pain in the neck. It doesn't matter. Nothing can stop the kids once they've sniffed the scent of another crime in the making. (Of course, sometimes they are simply smelling pizza.) Pizza is what this story is about. Pizza and a bad case of the flu.

As ten-year-old T.J. Booker rolled over in bed one morning, he knew exactly what he was smelling. The sharp mix of ammonia and pine made his nose twitch. In another second, his dark eyes popped open. "Get out of here with that stuff!" yelled the thin black boy, sitting bolt upright in bed. "Are you crazy? Why are you spraying disinfectant all over my room?"

"I don't want your flu germs," explained T.J.'s twelve-year-old foster brother, sandy-haired Jimmy Locke.

T.J. rubbed his eyes sleepily, then ran a hand through his short, black hair. "Don't come in here if you don't want my germs."

"I need to borrow a pair of socks," said Jimmy. He moved across T.J.'s room and continued to spray ahead of him, shielding his brown eyes with his hand. Jimmy looked as though he were creating a force field between himself and T.J.'s flu germs.

T.J. coughed and jumped out of bed. He grabbed the can out of Jimmy's hand. "Cut that out!"

A pair of green eyes and a button nose peeked around the bedroom door. "What's going on?" asked eight-year-old Dottie Brewster, the youngest of the family. She shook her head of red curls. "Boy! It stinks in here."

"It didn't until Mr. Clean here decided to

wage a war on germs," said T.J., stashing the can under his pillow.

The next to pop his head into the room was eleven-year-old Lee Van Tho. "Are my white sneakers in here?" asked the wiry Vietnamese boy, his eyes darting around the room in search of his sneakers.

"Nope," said T.J.

"Bet they are," said Lee. "Remember, you borrowed them as part of that disguise you were working on. The one where you wanted to look like a famous tennis star."

"Oh, yeah, sorry," T.J. apologized. He got off the bed and began to dig through his over-stuffed closet for the sneakers. Strange things flew over his shoulder as he dug. A curly red wig. Oversized sunglasses. A plastic duck bill. An old, fringed lampshade. Hats of every description—a straw hat, a sailor's cap, a base-ball cap, and several others. Next came a mon-ster mask, flippers, a red cape, a fake moustache. Jimmy, Dottie, and Lee didn't even give the collection a second glance. They knew that as the Clues Kids' resident master of disguise, T.J. needed those things.

"Here they are," said T.J., finally pulling the sneakers from the back of his closet.

"Smile!"

T.J. looked up and saw Jay, Jimmy's twin, facing him with his camera. He snapped a pic-ture of T.J. sitting on his small mountain of costumes holding Lee's sneakers. "That'll be great!" said Jay as the photo slid out of the camera. "I'm doing a project for school, a photo biography of my family."

Jay was the shutterbug of the group. He loved to take pictures, especially if they were of criminals in the act of committing crimes.

"Don't show the Klinks that picture," warned sensible Dottie. "They'll faint if they see that T.J.'s closet is a disaster area."

Phil and Patty Klink were the kids' foster parents. T.J., Dottie, Lee, Jimmy, and Jay would still be living in the children's shelter if the Klinks hadn't come along. They gave the five children a home where they could be part of a big, happy family.

"Don't worry," said T.J., cramming everything back into his closet. "The Chief would have pity on a poor, sick kid."

"Maybe, but you're not going to be sick forever," said Dottie. "And then it will be clean-up time. You know how the Chief feels about orderliness."

"The Chief" was the kids' nickname for Phil Klink. In fact, practically everyone in Dozerville called him the Chief. That could have been because he was a take-charge kind of person who always seemed to know what to do in any situation. It could have been, but it wasn't. It was because he had been the chief of police for many years until he retired.

At that moment, the Chief appeared in T.J.'s doorway. He was still in his robe, and his wavy white hair was mussed from sleeping. "It's eight-fifteen," he announced. "Let's get downstairs and have some breakfast before you leave for school."

"Chief, can I go to school today?" asked T.J.

"He must be insane with fever," teased Jimmy. "He *wants* to go to school?"

Even T.J. was stunned by the sound of his own words. He couldn't believe he was asking to go to school, either. But after two days of being stuck in his room, school suddenly sounded good to him.

Phil Klink crossed the room and felt T.J.'s forehead with his large, rough hand. "You're still warm," he said. "I'm afraid you're home for the rest of the week. No sense rushing back and then having a relapse."

T.J. moaned and fell back flat on his bed. "Phooey," he grumbled.

The Chief sniffed the air like a bloodhound on a case. "Do I smell disinfectant?" he asked.

"I was de-germing the room," Jimmy admitted.

The Chief rubbed his short, white beard. "I'd say you got a little carried away," he said. Phil pulled up T.J.'s window, being careful not to jostle the telescope that stood in front of it. "This room needs to be aired out." Although it was a beautiful spring day, a cool breeze made its way into the room. "I'll get you an extra blanket so you don't get chilled," said the Chief. "I think there are some in your closet."

He turned toward the closet. Dottie jumped in front of him before he could touch the door-knob. "I'll get him a blanket, Chief," she said. "You go on down and have your breakfast."

"Okay. Thank you, Dottie," he said, walking out of the room. "Everyone except T.J.—downstairs in five minutes. I don't want you late for school."

The kids moved. They knew that when the Chief said five minutes, he meant it.

"Bye, T.J.," Dottie said, handing him a blanket.

"Bye." T.J. waved to her sadly.

"Don't feel bad. You're not missing anything. We haven't noticed a single crime being committed since you've been sick."

"Jimmy said you were trailing a car thief the other day," T.J. said enviously.

Dottie crinkled her mouth into an expression of disgust. "It was just old Mr. Snodgrass. When we saw him fiddling with the lock of a car, Jimmy decided he was trying to steal it. We followed him all the way to the locksmith's before he noticed us. He chased us back down the block waving his cane and yelling."

"What was he yelling?" T.J. asked.

Dottie rolled her eyes. "He shouted, 'Can't a man lock himself out of his car in peace?' It was so embarrassing."

"You guys thought that old man was a car thief?" T.J. asked in disbelief. "You must be getting desperate for some excitement."

Dottie shrugged. "I told you, it's been very boring. We were just hoping."

"You're not as bored as I am," T.J. complained. He sat up and peeked into the telescope in front of his window. "The Chief set this up for me. He said it would help me while away the hours.

I've been looking through this thing for days, and nothing interesting has happened."

"Maybe today will be different," said Dottie cheerfully. "Good luck." She waved and disappeared through the doorway.

Just as he'd been for the last two days, T.J. found himself all alone. He worked on sketches for some new disguises until Mrs. Klink brought him a tray of steaming pancakes and some orange juice for breakfast. "How's my little patient today?" she asked, fluffing up T.J.'s pillow behind him.

"Bored," T.J. grumbled.

Mrs. Klink studied him with her sparkly blue eyes and placed a soft hand on his forehead. "Still hot," she said. She pulled a bottle of children's aspirin from the pocket of the apron she wore over her pants. "Here you go," she said, spilling two pink pills out into her palm. "These will help your fever."

After Mrs. Klink left, T.J. realized how sick he still felt when he could only eat half the pancakes. He usually wolfed down an entire stack, and then asked for seconds.

He put the tray down on the floor and turned to the telescope. The view from his window at the front of the house wasn't all that interesting. Across Webb Avenue were two more big old houses like the Klinks'. On the next street, T.J. could see a row of stores. Joe's Hardware was the first. Danny's Deli Delights was next to that. Then came Lady Lou's House of Clothes.

In the past two days the most interesting sight

he'd seen was Amos Noteworthy, the town census taker, walking down the street with his pet chimp, Boswell. Amos seemed to believe that Boswell was almost human, and dressed him in a hat and coat.

T.J. gazed into the telescope and scanned the block. Through the magnified round circle he could see the drivers in two cars that passed by. He saw Joe Sawyer put a "Sale" sign up on the front window of his hardware store. A delivery boy wearing sunglasses, a red baseball cap, and a red cotton jacket rode down the street on his bike. In the bike's basket was a large box of pizza.

It's awfully early to be delivering pizza, T.J. thought. *It's still breakfast time.* T.J. imagined an oatmeal pizza with plenty of butter. His stomach didn't like that thought. He moved his telescope a bit. A spotted dog ambled up the street.

But wait! T.J. moved the telescope back to the delivery boy. Something strange was happening. The boy turned into the alley between the hardware store and the deli. T.J. watched as the boy leaned his bike against the wall and dropped the box of pizza into a garbage can in the alley. Then he left his bike behind and walked off.

T.J. sat back and rubbed his eyes. It didn't add up. Why would the delivery boy toss away his pizza? And why would he leave his bike behind?

Here, at last, was something interesting.

He looked back into the telescope. What he

saw next amazed and puzzled him even more. The delivery boy came back up the alley. He fished the pizza out of the garbage, and then rode off on his bike.

The crime alert in T.J.'s mind sounded, loud and clear. He smacked his hands together excitedly. Something crooked was going on out there and—flu or no flu—he would find a way to get to the bottom of it!

C·H·A·P·T·E·R
2

"**A** case, at last," said Jimmy that afternoon after school. The kids were all sitting on top of T.J.'s bed listening to him tell the story of the strange delivery boy.

"I have one question," Jay said to T.J. "What happened to your leg?"

T.J. patted his right leg, which he'd wrapped in a papier-mâché cast. It had taken him two hours after lunch. "It's a new disguise I'm working on," he explained. "Being sick gave me the idea of working on a whole new series of sick-people disguises. No one would suspect a sick person of being a detective."

"Are you going to walk around with that thing on your leg all the time?" asked Dottie.

"Of course not," replied T.J. "When it's completely dry, I'm going to cut it open so I can slip it on and off."

"Let's get back to the case at hand," said Jimmy. He hopped off the bed and paced dramatically back and forth, his hands clasped behind his back. "I have it!" he said, spreading his arms wide. "The delivery boy is a spy. There

17

are secret documents in that pizza box—maybe they're baked right into the pizza itself."

"Could be," Lee agreed. "If I had been here I could have run down into the alley and dusted that box for fingerprints before the guy came and picked it up again." Lee was always ready to use his fingerprinting kit to help solve crimes. Unfortunately, Lee often wound up with more ink smudged on his face than anywhere else.

"If only I'd been there with my camera, I could have photographed the spy in the act," said Jay. "Instead, I was stuck in a spelling bee while the safety of this country was being threatened by enemy agents."

Dottie gave Jay a funny look. "We don't know that the safety—"

"How do you think I felt?" said T.J. excitedly. "I was stuck here. If I wasn't sick, I could have disguised myself as a bike racer and followed him."

"Wait a minute," said Dottie. "You're all forgetting one thing. If the guy was passing secret documents, why would he drop them off and then pick them up himself?"

The kids sat silently and thought about that for a moment. "Good question," said Jay at last. "There's got to be a reason." The kids sat and thought some more. Then they turned to one another and shrugged their shoulders. They were stumped.

"I think the first step is to find out what pizza parlor the delivery boy works for," Dottie suggested.

The boys nodded seriously. They were serious because they knew this wouldn't be easy—not with twenty-six pizza parlors in Dozerville. "Did he have anything written on his jacket?" Jimmy asked T.J.

T.J. scrunched up his face, trying to remember. "I think there was some writing on his jacket, but I couldn't make it out."

"If you see him again, try to read it," Jimmy instructed. "It's going to take forever to go to all the pizza parlors and interview all the owners."

"We won't have to," said Lee. "We just have to narrow it down to the pizza parlors whose delivery boys ride bikes and wear red jackets and caps."

"I think a lot of them wear the same thing," said Jay glumly.

"There's only one way to find out," Jimmy said, heading for the door. "Let's get started. Who knows? The future of the free world might depend on us."

"Oh, brother." Dottie sighed.

Jay, Dottie, and Lee followed him out of the room. "Hey!" called T.J. "What about me?"

"Man your post," Jimmy told him. "You are home base, central headquarters. You're the eyes and backbone of this operation. We depend on you to keep a ceaseless watch on Webb Avenue and the surrounding area. We depend on you to—"

"Oh, be quiet!" said Dottie. Jimmy was the talker of the group. When the Clues Kids were in a jam, sometimes Jimmy could talk their way out of it. The trouble was, he didn't know when to *stop* talking. "T.J., just watch the street and hope the delivery guy comes back," Dottie said.

"Okay," T.J. agreed, turning to his telescope.

The rest of the kids ran downstairs, creating a loud clatter on the wooden steps. They raced for the front door.

"Whoa!" called Mrs. Klink. She was kneeling in the front hallway, putting a leash on Snoop, the family's floppy-eared basset hound. "Where are all of you charging off to? I was going to ask one of you to walk Snoop."

The kids exchanged glances. They couldn't take Snoop into the pizza parlors with them. "Can we do it later?" asked Lee. "We're sort of busy now."

"Busy with what?" Mrs. Klink asked.

The kids didn't know how to answer. They knew Mrs. Klink didn't like them to get involved in solving crimes. It wasn't that she wanted to spoil their fun. It was that she worried about them getting hurt. And, since they *had* almost gotten hurt on several occasions, there was no point in telling her not to worry.

"Ummm . . . we've decided to take a survey of all the pizza parlors in Dozerville," Jimmy said. That wasn't a lie. Not exactly.

Mrs. Klink's eyes narrowed suspiciously. She rumpled her short red hair with her hand. "Is there any particular reason for conducting this survey?" she asked.

"It's a public service," said Jay. That wasn't exactly a lie, either. Not exactly.

"Well, all right," she said slowly, still sounding doubtful. "I'll walk Snoop, but don't eat too much pizza. You'll spoil your supper."

"We won't," the kids assured her, all at the same time, as they scrambled out the door. They grabbed their bikes, which were leaning against the side of the big old wooden house.

"What's our first stop?" asked Lee.

"Pino's Pizzeria is the closest," Jimmy suggested. "Might as well start there and keep going."

The kids jumped on their bikes and raced down the street toward Pino's, which was two blocks away. "Wait for me!" cried Dottie, who couldn't pedal as fast as the others. By the time she caught up with them, the boys were already chaining their bikes to the rack in front of Pino's.

"Is this combination three-two-six, or six-two-three?" Lee muttered as he fiddled with his combination lock. He tried one, and then the other. Neither worked.

Jay stood over him and shook his head. "Don't tell me you've forgotten the combination to another lock! This is the fifth lock you've had to throw away this year," he said. "Why don't you write the combination down somewhere?"

"I do," said Lee, "but then I lose the paper I wrote it down on."

"I guess you'll have to stay out here with your bike," said Jimmy.

"No way!" Lee refused. "This is Dozerville, not a big city. The Klinks don't even lock their front door, except when they're out. No one will take my bike."

"I'm locking mine, anyway," said Dottie. "I've never had a bike as nice as this one before. I don't want to take a chance on anything happening to it."

"Come on," said Lee. "My bike will be okay. Let's go inside and see what we can find out."

The pizza parlors in Dozerville came in all shapes and sizes. Pino's was long and narrow, with a hand-painted mural on the wall that showed a scene of the canals in Venice. Men in curvy gondolas pushed their boats with long poles.

"Could you imagine all the streets in Dozerville being filled with water like in Venice?" asked Dottie, looking up at the mural.

"I wouldn't like it," said Jay. "It would make it kind of hard to ride your bike, for one thing."

Dottie giggled. "You'd have to put water skis on the tires and hire one of those men with the boats to pull you along."

A man came out from behind the counter. "We won't ask him directly," Jay whispered to the others. "We don't want to alert him in case he's the head of the spy ring."

Jimmy stepped in front of the group and sidled up to the counter. "You know what?" he asked the man boldly. "You look like you could use a delivery boy."

"I don't think—" the man began.

"But I only want to work here if your delivery boys wear red jackets," Jimmy pressed.

"They do wear red jackets, but—"

"And red caps," Jimmy added quickly. "I can't deliver pizza without a red cap."

"Our fellows do wear red jackets and red caps, but—"

"Just one second," Jimmy told the man. He ran back to Dottie, Jay, and Lee, who were hanging back near the tables. "I think this is our guy," he said. "The red caps, the jackets. The way he doesn't want me to work for him. I think we're on to something here."

"Are you sure?" asked Dottie, unconvinced.

"Trust me," said Jimmy. He walked back to the man, swaggering as he moved, trying to look tough. "So," he said, slouching against the counter. "Why is it you don't want me to deliver for you?"

"I'm sorry, but I simply don't—" the man started to answer.

"Afraid I'll get too close to your operation? Think I'll see too much?" challenged Jimmy. He was sure this man was the head of operations. Maybe if he could make the man nervous, he'd slip and reveal a clue. "The police might be interested to know why you don't want me to work here. I think I'll give them a call."

"Don't do that," said the man.

Jimmy was sure he had the man scared now. "Then tell me why you don't want me to work here."

The man creased his brow and looked at Jimmy as if he were crazy. "I don't think you'd be able to drive our delivery truck, son," he said.

A red blush of embarrassment started at Jimmy's ears and spread quickly across his entire face. "Oh, yes, well, there is that. I could drive. But I prefer not to. The police wouldn't let me, anyway," Jimmy stammered, backing away from the man.

The kids looked up and began to whistle, pretending they didn't know Jimmy. He glared at them. "Let's get out of here," he mumbled under his breath. Continuing to whistle, the kids followed Jimmy out of the pizzeria.

"I feel like such a jerk!" cried Jimmy once they were outside.

"That's nothing new," Lee teased. "Did you really have to cross-examine the guy?"

"I guess I was a little too eager," Jimmy admitted.

Jay patted his brother on the back. "Just calm down next time."

"Well, we can count Pino's out," Dottie said. "Their delivery guys drive trucks."

Jay looked at his red plastic wristwatch. The mouse's hands indicated it was three-fifteen. "I think we have time to check out one more pizzeria before *Cosmic Cop* comes on." *Cosmic Cop* was absolutely the kids' favorite TV show. Jay held his watch to his ear. "I think my watch might be a little slow. What time does yours say, Lee?"

Lee didn't answer. He was staring at the bikes. "Lee," Jay repeated. "Earth to Lee. Come in."

"What's wrong with this picture?" Lee asked, looking very unhappy.

Jimmy, Jay, and Dottie looked at the bike rack. It seemed okay to them. Then, all at once, they realized the problem. "Your bike is gone," said Jay.

Lee sighed, and his shoulders drooped. "You got it."

Dottie looked up one side of the street, Jimmy looked down the other. There was no one around. Whoever had taken Lee's bike was nowhere to be seen.

"That stinks!" Dottie cried.

"What kind of creep would do that?" Jay shouted angrily. He turned and put his hand on Lee's sagging shoulder. "Don't worry. If the Clues Kids can't find a missing bike, I don't know who can."

"That's right!" said Jimmy. "Who would have believed that yesterday we had no cases to solve—and now we have two mysteries on our hands!"

C·H·A·P·T·E·R
3

Sergeant Beasley leaned over his high desk and looked down at the kids. "Yes?" he asked pleasantly.

"We've come to report a stolen bike," Jimmy told him. The kids had decided that it wouldn't hurt to get a little help from the Dozerville police department on this one.

The heavyset police officer sighed. "Not another one!"

"You mean this has been happening to other kids?" asked Lee.

"We've had four bike thefts this week alone. We had three the week before that." Sergeant Beasley shook his head. "I don't know what's happening. The people of Dozerville used to be so honest."

"I bet most of them still are," said Jimmy. "Maybe it's just one or two people who are stealing all the bikes. What's the *modus operandi?*"

Sergeant Beasley looked confused.

"You know, the M.O., the method of operation," said Jimmy. *Modus operandi*—or M.O.

for short—was a term he'd picked up from watching TV detective shows. "Don't you know what that means?"

"I know," said the sergeant. "I just didn't know you knew."

"Sure he does," Dottie said. She looked up at Sergeant Beasley. "So how are the crooks stealing the bikes?"

"If we knew that, maybe we'd have a clue," said the sergeant. "So far, we don't know a thing. The bikes simply seem to vanish."

The kids gave Sergeant Beasley a description of Lee's bike and told him where it was stolen. They gave their address and phone number, in case the bicycle turned up.

"Have you recovered any of the stolen bikes?" asked Lee hopefully.

"Not a one," said the sergeant. "We'll look for your bike, young man, but I can't promise we'll find it."

A glum little group slowly walked their bikes home.

"Today sure has been a bust," said Jimmy when they reached the Klinks' house. "We don't know anything more about the pizza mystery, and now Lee's bike is gone."

"And," added Jay, checking his watch, "we've missed *Cosmic Cop*." The group groaned. No matter what else was happening, the kids usually assembled in front of the TV every day to see Cosmic Cop save the universe from destruction.

They'd especially wanted to see the show

today, because at the end of the last episode Cosmic was in great danger. He had chased the galaxy's craftiest thief, Stella Slick, to her hide-away on the planet Gaspar. Cosmic was about to step into Stella's pit of man-eating Hydra monsters . . . And now they'd never know what happened. (Naturally, they assumed Cosmic would escape, but seeing *how* he did it was the fun part.)

Glumly, they trudged up the creaky front steps. The screen door squeaked as Dottie pulled it open. "Here they are," they heard the Chief say from the dining room.

Mrs. Klink met them in the hall with her hands on her hips and a cross expression on her face. "It's about time," she said. "Supper's already on the table. Where have you kids been?"

"Sorry," they mumbled together.

When Mrs. Klink saw how sad they looked, her face lost its angry expression and a look of concern came into her eyes. "What's wrong?" she asked.

"My bike was stolen," Lee told her.

"Good gracious!" Mrs. Klink cried. "Who would have done such a thing?" Mrs. Klink thought the best of everyone. She was always doing things for the community, like planning programs to help those less fortunate than her-self. She did it because she liked people, and assumed everyone felt the same way she did. That's why it always took her by surprise when someone did something mean.

"That's crummy," said T.J. from the dining

room. He was already sitting next to the Chief at the table. He wore a blue robe, and his leg with the fake cast stuck out beside him, propped up on a separate chair. He'd tried to cut it off with scissors, but it proved too thick and hard. He was hoping he'd think of some other way of removing it.

"Wash up and come to the table," Mrs. Klink instructed them. "Tell us all about it while you eat. A good meal will make you feel a little better."

They sat down to a big supper of roast chicken with gravy, mashed potatoes, green beans, broccoli, and applesauce. Since the Chief was retired, he and Mrs. Klink shared the cooking. They could tell from the large quantities of food on the table that the Chief had prepared tonight's supper. He was a man who loved to eat.

At dinner, they gobbled down everything. Everything, that is, except the broccoli. That they dropped under the table. Snoop and Prowler, their black cat, sat under the table and were always happy to eat anything the kids didn't want. Well, almost anything. Broccoli wasn't their favorite food either.

Between mouthfuls, the kids told Mr. and Mrs. Klink how Lee's bike had disappeared. They also mentioned what Sergeant Beasley had told them about the rash of bike thefts. The Klinks listened quietly through most of the meal.

"We haven't had bike nabbers in Dozerville for almost forty years," said the Chief as he

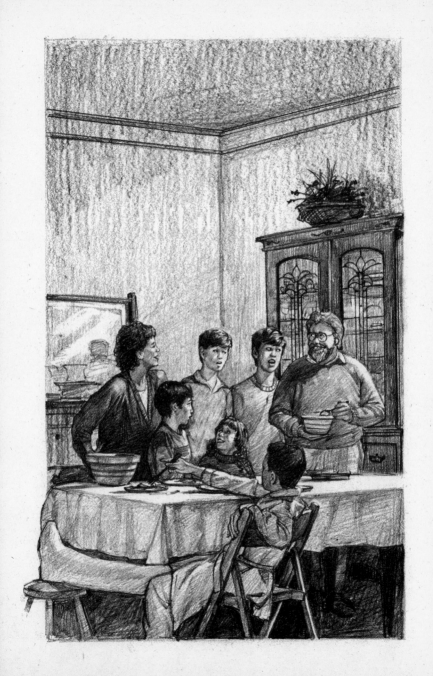

finished up the last of his chicken. "That was when Bunny Moses and Pinky O'Brian ran a ring of thieves from George Fenwick's chicken coop." The Chief sat back and chuckled at the memory. "I remember I took a group of officers up there after dark and—"

"You slipped a fox in the back door," said Jay enthusiastically.

"And the chickens went wild and started running all over the place," added Dottie.

"There were feathers everywhere!" said T.J.

"All the crooks were coughing and sneezing. They ran out of the chicken coop, and you were waiting there to nab them," Jimmy finished the story triumphantly.

The Chief smiled sheepishly. "It seems I've told this story before."

Mrs. Klink's eyes were twinkling with laughter. "It would seem so," she said. The Chief had certain favorite stories he liked to tell again and again. This was one of them. It didn't bother the kids, though. They never got tired of hearing them. Well—almost never.

"I wish someone would nab these guys," said Lee sadly. "I loved that bike."

Mrs. Klink got up to clear away dishes. That was the signal for everyone else (except for T.J., who was excused due to the flu) to do the same. "It won't replace a stolen bike or cure the flu," Mrs. Klink said as she scraped all the scraps onto one dish, "but I have something that should cheer you all up a bit. I'll show you when the dishes are done."

The kids were so eager to find out what the surprise was that they had the dining room cleared and the dishes done in a flash. When they were done, Mrs. Klink led them to the living room. She took a black video cassette from the top of the TV. "Today's episode of *Cosmic Cop*," she announced. "I taped it for you."

"Yeah!" the kids cheered. Dottie threw her arms around Mrs. Klink's waist gratefully. "Does Cosmic get out of Stella Slick's trap?" she asked.

"My lips are sealed. You'll have to see for yourselves," she replied, popping the cassette into the VCR. In seconds, *Cosmic Cop*'s electronic theme song filled the living room. T.J. was already propped up on the couch wrapped in a blanket, his fake cast stretched out in front of him. Lee pulled one of the pillows out from under T.J. and settled down on the floor. Dottie sat in her favorite spot, the Chief's big cozy chair. Jimmy and Jay wrestled over who would sit in Mrs. Klink's recliner, and wound up sharing it—Jimmy scrunched in the back and Jay curled at the foot.

They watched Cosmic, in his gold uniform with silver and black trim, battle the many-tentacled Hydra monsters. Stella Slick gloated from above the pit. She wasn't smiling when Cosmic used his special molecular divider ring to split himself into two people and make mincemeat (or in this case, Hydra meat) out of the monsters. He then fused back into one hero and leaped out of the pit with a mighty bound.

"Where are the jeweled gowns of Gaspar, you meteoric menace?" Cosmic demanded in his best voice.

"I'll never tell, you overgrown space scout!" Stella screamed. But after a few more insults, she did tell him where she'd hidden the fabulous gowns of Gaspar. Cosmic was about to return the gowns, when suddenly the red jewels on their hems began to glow. A beam shot out of one and hit Cosmic in the head and . . .

They'd have to tune in tomorrow to find out what happened next.

"That was a great one!" said Jimmy. The kids agreed—all except Lee. He seemed lost in his own thoughts. "You weren't even watching?" Jimmy said to Lee.

"What? . . . Oh, no, I guess not," Lee admitted.

"Boy, you must really be depressed about your bike to not even watch *Cosmic Cop*," said Dottie.

"I am," admitted Lee.

"Hey, you guys never told me what you found out about the pizza deliverer," said T.J.

"Forget about that," said Lee. "Finding out who took my bike is more important."

"More important than all of North America?" T.J. challenged him. "More important than the whole free world? These guys are spies, remember?"

"We don't know that for sure," said Lee. "All we know for sure is that my bike is gone."

"Hold on," said Jimmy. "If you two had been paying attention to *Cosmic Cop* you'd know what to do. We have to split into two indestructible forces so we can cover twice as much territory."

"Oh, sure," Jay said rudely. He pretended to search his pants pocket. "Now, where did I put my molecular divider ring?"

Jimmy used his feet to push Jay off the end of the recliner. "Lee and I will try to track down the bike thieves. Dottie and Jay can go after the pizza spies."

"What about me?" asked T.J. He was getting really sick of being left out. "And don't tell me I'm in charge of headquarters!"

"You're not headquarters anymore," Jimmy told him, getting off the recliner. "You're the eyes of this operation. Keeping careful watch through your telescope, never resting at your post, you survey the neighborhood. Nothing escapes your keen sight, heightened by a high-tech telescope. And even in the darkest shadows—"

Dottie interrupted with a loud sigh. "Just keep looking out the window, T.J., and see if anything strange turns up."

"Okay," T.J. agreed. He suddenly felt very tired. Dragging his blanket behind him like a long cape, he got off the couch and hobbled on his fake cast toward the stairs. "Good night, everybody," he said. "Tomorrow is going to be a long day. I have to figure out how to get this darned cast off my leg. And . . ." he started up the stairs, "this *private eye* has to watch for a spy."

C·H·A·P·T·E·R
4

"**M**y clothes are starting to smell like pizza," complained Dottie. She and Jay had met after school and immediately began checking out the local pizza parlors. They started with The Crust Is Us, the newest pizzeria in town, and kept going from there. They'd just left Everything On It, and were walking their bikes across the street to The One and Only Original LaCosta's Pizza Palace.

So far, they'd had no luck. The delivery boys either drove cars, wore blue, or wore their own clothes. Spicy Tomatoes pizzeria refused to deliver, and the delivery boys at Miss Toni's Pizza Parlor wore pink coveralls. Actually, they were delivery *girls*, which eliminated them as suspects. So far, the kids hadn't found a single red jacket or baseball cap in the bunch.

Finally, Dottie and Jay entered Original LaCosta's. It was a large, clean place with red plastic tables and mirrors on the walls. Potted ferns hung from the ceiling, and a big sign over the counter said, "I was here first!" When they saw the sign, Dottie and Jay remembered that there were two other stores in town named LaCosta's.

They told the owners of the pizzerias they were doing a study on local businesses for school. Jay took photos of all the pizzerias and the people who worked there, just in case they overlooked something during their visit. Jay checked his camera. He had ten pictures left on the roll of film.

They walked to the front counter where a short, bald man in a red-striped jacket was tossing pizza dough. Thinking that it would make a neat photo, Jay held the camera to his eye and got ready to shoot. The automatic flash on the camera popped up. Jay framed the man and the dough in his lens and then—*click! Flash!*

"What the—?" The man saw the flash just as he tossed the pizza. He turned toward Jay, blinking.

Plop!

Down came the pizza dough—right on top of his bald head.

Dottie and Jay looked at one another with panicked eyes. Then they heard a low chuckle coming from the man underneath the pizza dough. His shoulders were shaking with laughter as he stood there with the dough completely covering his face. It was such a funny sight that Dottie and Jay had to cover their mouths with their hands to keep from laughing.

Slowly, the man peeled the gooey dough off his face. "I've been throwing dough for thirty years," he chuckled. "That's never happened to me, but I always knew someday it would."

"Sorry," Jay apologized. "I should have warned you."

"No problem," the man told him as he wiped his face with the red apron he wore under his striped jacket. "So, what'll you kids have?"

Dottie and Jay said they didn't want to eat. They'd come to interview the owner about his business. "Well, I'm the owner," he told them, "the original Manny LaCosta."

He served two customers slices and sodas, and then turned back to the kids. "If you want to know about the pizza business in this town, you've come to the right place. Believe it or not, there was a time when there was only one pizza place in Dozerville, and this was it. Back east, where I come from, there was a pizzeria on every corner. There was too much competition. So I said to myself, go west, young man. I set up this place and the folks here went crazy over it. Some of them had never even tasted pizza before. But, like a noodlehead, I wrote to my family and told them how great I was doing."

"Why was writing to your family a noodle-head thing to do?" asked Dottie.

"Because, little girl, the next thing I know, my cousin Vinnie LaCosta is out here setting up shop. I say, 'Okay, Vinnie, there's enough business for both of us.' So what does that anchovy-brain do? He writes to his half-brother, Carlo LaCosta, who comes zooming out here with a truckload of tomatoes. So now we've got three LaCosta's Pizzerias

in one little town. But does it stop there? As you know, it doesn't. Carlo writes to his buddy from the army, a guy named Marty Kelly, and *he* comes out and sets up a pizza place, and so on from there, until now we have twenty-six pizza parlors in Dozerville. And a twenty-seventh going up as we speak. Luckily, people in Dozerville are the pizza-eatingest bunch I've ever seen."

"That's very interesting," said Jay sincerely. "It all began right here."

"This very spot," said Manny LaCosta.

"Does it bother you that there are so many other pizza parlors in town?" asked Dottie.

Manny LaCosta slapped the counter angrily. "You know what bothers me? My own relatives bother me! All right, I understand why they called their pizzerias LaCosta's. I think they could have come up with something different, but, okay, they're also LaCostas. They're entitled. But they copy every other blessed thing I do. When I introduced my spinach pies, they had spinach pies the next week. When my delivery guys started wearing red—"

"Your delivery boys wear red jackets?" Jay interrupted.

"And red caps. They copied that, too," Manny told them.

Dottie and Jay looked at one another. Finally, they might be on to something. "Do they ride bikes?" Dottie asked.

Manny nodded. "And so do the guys who deliver for the other two LaCosta's. Here comes one of my guys now."

Dottie and Jay turned to see a delivery boy coming through the front door. Sure enough, he had on a red jacket, a red baseball cap, and—as T.J. had mentioned—he wore dark sunglasses.

"Ray," Manny called to him. "Come here and meet two kids who are doing a report on our business for school."

Ray didn't take off his sunglasses, even though he'd come inside. He hesitated a moment before coming over, then he grunted hello to Dottie and Jay. The little bell over the front door of the shop rang as a customer entered. Ray jumped at the sound and looked over his shoulder nervously.

"What took you so long on that last run?" Manny asked pleasantly as Ray handed him the money from the last delivery. "You left at three, it's already three twenty-five."

"Ummm . . . got lost," Ray answered.

Manny chuckled. "I forgot you just moved into town." Using a smooth, wide wooden paddle, he took a pie from the oven and slid it into a box. "This one goes to the Sloats. I'll write down the address on the box."

It seemed that Ray was barely listening. "Yeah, sure thing," he replied absently.

Manny penciled in the address and gave the box to Ray. Without another word, he took the box and headed for the door.

"What did you think of that guy?" Jay whispered to Dottie while Manny was busy with a customer.

"I thought he was creepy," Dottie answered.

"Creepy enough to be a spy?" asked Jay. Dottie nodded. "I think so, too," said Jay. "Let's follow him."

"Thanks, Mr. LaCosta," Dottie called over her shoulder as she and Jay raced to the door. "We have to hurry home to get this report done."

"Sure thing," Manny said, waving. "Come anytime."

In a minute, Dottie and Jay were out on the street. Ray was gone. "He can't have gone far," said Dottie, unchaining her bike. "Let's try to find him."

Jay and Dottie pedaled down the street at top speed. Jay turned right at the corner, and Dottie kept going straight. They met up again in front of Original LaCosta's.

"Boy," said Jay, wiping sweat from his brow, "for a guy who's new in town, that Ray sure knew how to disappear in a flash!"

Dottie wiped her damp brow. "That's okay," she said. "We can come back tomorrow."

"Yeah," Jay agreed. "And tomorrow we'll be ready for him."

C·H·A·P·T·E·R
5

*D*ottie and Jay burst in the front door just as Jimmy and Lee were settling down to watch *Cosmic Cop*. The show had only been on a few minutes. (T.J. had fallen asleep upstairs, and Mrs. Klink didn't want him awakened. She was taping the episode for him.) They were dying to tell their news about Ray the delivery boy, but Jimmy shushed them when they tried to talk. Cosmic was being hurled into another dimension by the beam that shot out of the gem on the hem of the gown of Gaspar. Jimmy and Lee didn't want to miss a second of it.

In minutes, Jay and Dottie were also wrapped up in Cosmic's next adventure. They almost forgot all about Original LaCosta's pizzeria and its nasty delivery boy.

"So?" asked Jimmy at the commercial break.

Dottie and Jay looked at him blankly. "So what?" asked Jay.

"So what were you going to tell us about the delivery guys?"

"Oh, yeah." Jay had been sprawled on the

floor in front of the TV. Now he sat up straight and told Jimmy and Lee how they suspected Ray of being the person T.J. had spotted. He also told them how Ray had disappeared on his bike just minutes after leaving the pizzeria.

"He's got to be the one," Lee agreed. "He even had sunglasses on, like the guy T.J. saw. I wonder what he's up to."

"Dinner!" called Mrs. Klink from the hall.

Suddenly there was a loud clatter and the thumping sound of someone hitting the wall. The kids looked at one another, their eyes wide with fright. "It's coming from the cellar!" cried Lee. With Mrs. Klink in the lead, they ran to the cellar door at the end of the hallway. Slowly, Mrs. Klink opened the door.

"Darn that Benny!" growled the Chief from the bottom of the cellar stairs where he stood, dusting himself off. "I told him to fix those top steps. What good is a repairman if he doesn't repair things? I told him someone was going to get hurt—and whenever I say that, it always, *always* turns out to be me who gets hurt."

The kids looked down the narrow stairway and saw that the tops of the third and fourth steps were missing. They'd gone sliding to the bottom of the staircase—along with the Chief.

"I'll call him in the morning, dear," Mrs. Klink said. "Are you all right?"

The Chief smoothed his blue sweater and picked up the two loose steps. "I'm a little bruised," he said climbing the stairs once again, "but I'll survive. You kids stay out of the cellar until Benny comes to fix these steps."

When he reached the third and fourth steps, he placed the wooden slats where they belonged. Then he stepped over them and joined the others in the hallway. Mrs. Klink patted him on the back. "Poor thing," she said sympathetically.

"Darn!" said the Chief. "I forgot—the reason I went down there was to bring up some pickles to have with the pork chops and sauerkraut tonight."

"We don't need them," said Mrs. Klink. "Come and eat."

"I'll go get them," volunteered Dottie, who loved pickles, and hated sauerkraut.

The Chief put his big hand on her shoulder. "It's much too dangerous. Come on, let's eat."

Mrs. Klink brought a dinner plate up to T.J., and then they all sat down to dinner. The Chief was still a bit out of sorts after his tumble down the stairs. But—true to Mrs. Klink's theory—a good meal made him feel better. Soon he was telling them about the time when he'd ridden a bike through the Swiss Alps on a special mission.

He stopped talking and looked at Lee. "I'm sorry, son. I forgot to ask you if there was any news on your bike."

"Not on my bike exactly," Lee told him, "but Jimmy and I heard in school that two other kids had their bikes taken last week."

"We went and talked to the kids, and it was

just the same as with Lee's bike," Jimmy added. "One minute the bike was there. The next minute it was gone. No one saw a thing."

"And those two kids had chained their bikes, too," said Lee. "Whoever did it cut the locks." This information had made Lee feel a little better. He'd been blaming himself for not chaining his bike.

Lee was starting to give up on ever seeing his bike again. It was a new blue and silver five-speed. The Klinks had bought it for him when he first came to live with them, and—next to his fingerprinting kit—it was his most treasured possession. Now he might never see it again.

Dottie was becoming depressed, too. But for a different reason. Snoop and Prowler refused to eat the sauerkraut she offered them under the table. She couldn't just toss it on the carpet, so she put it back on her plate. There's nothing more depressing than a plateful of cold sauerkraut staring up at you.

After dishes, the kids ran upstairs. They were supposed to be doing homework, but they stopped a minute in front of T.J.'s door. "He can't *still* be sleeping," said Jay.

Quietly opening the door, Jay peeked in. In the dimly lit room, he could see that T.J.'s dinner plate remained untouched at the side of his bed. The lump under the covers, which Jay assumed was T.J., didn't move. Jay was worried. Why was T.J. so still? "He must be sicker than we thought," he said to the others, gulping hard.

"Poor T.J.," said Dottie.

Wordlessly, the kids crept into the room. Although the floorboards creaked under their feet, T.J. didn't stir. They gathered at the foot of his bed and gazed down fondly at the boy, who slept with the covers pulled over his head.

Suddenly the cover flipped down off T.J.'s face, and there, in the bed before them, was a mummy monster completely wrapped in white strips except for two closed eyes. In a second, the eyes snapped open and stared at them.

"Aaaaahhhh!" The kids screamed and jumped back across the room toward the door.

The mummy rose in the bed and swung its legs around. Then it held its belly and fell back on the bed hooting with laughter—a very familiar laughter.

"T.J.!" yelled Dottie, snapping on the bedroom light. "That wasn't funny."

Jimmy, Jay, and Lee pounced onto his bed and batted him with pillows. "Hey, watch it," chuckled T.J. as Lee swatted him. "I'm sick, you know."

"What was the big idea of scaring us like that?" asked Dottie, punching T.J. in the arm.

T.J. pulled the white strips from his face. In the light the kids could see that he was completely wrapped in toilet paper. "This is part of my sick people disguises series," he said happily.

"A mummy isn't sick," Jimmy informed him. "A mummy is dead. Old and dead."

"I'm not supposed to be a mummy," said T.J. "I was trying to look like someone who was in

a skiing accident and has a cast on his body from head to foot." T.J. tapped one paper-wrapped leg and it made a hollow sound. "As long as I still have this thing on, I figured I'd go for the full effect."

"Why don't you tear that dumb thing off, already?" said Jay.

"No way," T.J. objected. "I thought I could cut it with scissors and just slip out of it, but since it won't cut, I have another plan. I'm going to wait for Benny to come over with his tool box. He has a pair of wire clippers that should do the trick."

"Why don't you ask the Chief?" Jay suggested. "He has every kind of tool in his workshop in the barn."

"Everything except wire clippers," said T.J. "He told me he lent them to Benny last week."

"How do you know Benny is supposed to come again?" Lee challenged.

"He's here all the time," said T.J. He was right. There was always something that needed to be fixed in the Klinks' big old house. And though the Chief was very handy, there was more work than one person could manage alone.

"You're in luck," Dottie told T.J. "Mrs. Klink is going to call Benny to fix the cellar stairs."

"See," said T.J.

"It must have taken you all day to wrap your-self up in that stuff," said Jimmy. "Did you manage to look through your telescope at all?"

T.J.'s expression grew serious. "I have big news. I wanted to tell you guys this right away, but I fell asleep. You wouldn't think it, but it's tiring wrapping yourself in toilet paper."

"That's your big news?" snapped Jay impatiently.

"No, no. I saw him again. The delivery guy with the jacket and hat stopped in the alley and did the exact same thing as the other day. He ditched the pizza, got off the bike, and then came back."

Jay's eyes lit up. "Dottie and I know who he is," he told T.J. excitedly. "He works for Original LaCosta's. His name's Ray."

T.J. flipped back on the bed and shook his arms and legs happily. "All right! This case is finally getting somewhere." He rolled over on the bed. "We have a suspect now, and a pattern."

"And an M.O.," Jimmy added.

"Right," agreed T.J., not quite remembering what an M.O. was. "We know what this guy does, and we know that today he did it between three and three twenty-five. Now we have to figure out why he's doing this."

"Wait a minute," said Dottie. "Are you sure about the time?"

"I looked at my watch. It was definitely three twenty-five."

Dottie sighed. "Ray's not the person you spotted."

"He's got to be, Dottie," Jay argued. "He fits the description. He's creepy and acts suspicious."

Dottie shook her head. "He was also in Original LaCosta's with us at exactly three twenty-five."

Jay was silent. He knew Dottie was right, as usual. Finally he turned toward the window. "Then that means the real spy," Jay said softly, "is still out there."

C·H·A·P·T·E·R
6

"*T*his is great!" said Lee as he and Jimmy bounded down the front steps of Wrighter Elementary School on Friday. It was only one o'clock, but the students had the afternoon off. The teachers were attending a special seminar given by a local dentist. The topic was: Pizza—Fun Food or Tooth Time Bomb?

A warm spring breeze was blowing. Clusters of green and yellow buds seemed to have popped up on the tree branches overnight. It was a wonderful day to be free from school for a few extra hours.

Lee's happy mood faded as they reached the bottom of the stairs. That's when he remembered what he and the others had planned to do today after school: continue to search for the mysterious delivery boy. Since Ray couldn't possibly have been in two places at once, they decided they'd have to look for a new suspect.

Normally, Lee would have been excited about this, but working on this case meant that they

had more or less given up on finding his bike. There just weren't any clues to follow.

"Where are we supposed to meet Dottie and Jay?" Lee asked. Jimmy didn't seem to hear him. His wide brown eyes narrowed as he watched something in the schoolyard with great interest.

The schoolyard was off to the side of the school building. Lee followed Jimmy's gaze and saw one of their classmates, a short, red-haired boy named Billy Whinner, running toward the school bike rack, screaming hysterically. Something in his tone told Lee that Billy wasn't kidding around.

"Come on," said Jimmy, and the two boys raced toward the schoolyard. As they approached, a young man wearing sunglasses sped toward them on a bike, pedaling at top speed. The fake foxtail attached to the back seat flew out straight in the breeze.

"He's stealing my bike!" Billy shrieked.

The bike thief was almost next to them. Jimmy and Lee ran into his path, but he swerved and darted out into the street. Nimble and quick, Lee sprinted out onto the street after him.

HONK! A horn blared in Lee's ear. He turned to see a van bearing down on him. Suddenly he felt a thud, and his feet were off the ground. Then he hit the pavement hard.

When he dared to open his eyes, he breathed deeply. He hadn't been hit, thanks to Jimmy, who had come flying at Lee and knocked him out of the way of the van. Now the two of them lay sprawled in the street.

The van had screeched to a halt. A man, gasping and pale as chalk, jumped down from the driver's seat. "Are you kids okay?" he asked.

Lee got to his feet slowly. His arm was scraped and his hip hurt, but he was in one piece. Jimmy, too, felt for broken bones and didn't find any.

When the man saw that they were all right, he became furious and hollered about how crazy they were. "I'm sorry," Lee apologized. He knew the man had every right to be angry.

"Be careful next time," Jimmy scolded Lee after the man drove away. "That was a dumb thing to do."

"I know," said Lee. "Thanks, Jimmy. I'd be in the Dozerville Hospital Emergency Room right now if it wasn't for you."

"Forget it," said Jimmy. "Let's go talk to Billy."

They headed back to the schoolyard. When Billy saw them approach, his face fell. "You let them get away," he said.

"I didn't see you chasing him," Jimmy pointed out.

"You were closer," said Billy in a low, complaining voice. Billy Whinner pronounced his last name "winner," but sometimes the kids called him whiner. At the moment, Jimmy and Lee could understand why. "I couldn't get there fast enough, but you could have. I just got that foxtail, too." Looking like the most forlorn person in the world, he held up a chain that had been cut clean through. "I locked it and everything."

"I know how you feel," said Lee. "Someone took my bike, too."

"Hey!" Dottie and Jay hurried toward them. "I got a picture!" Jay shouted excitedly. "Dottie and I were coming to meet you and we saw you guys almost collide with the van. Then I realized you were after that guy on the bike, so I took a quick shot as he zoomed past us. I hope it's not too blurry. Are you all right?"

Jimmy and Lee nodded. They told Dottie and Jay about the most recent bike theft.

"That guy was wearing sunglasses," Dottie thought out loud. "Ray had on sunglasses."

"Dottie, look around you," said Jay. "It's a sunny day. I see at least five people with sunglasses on right now. It's not exactly a clue."

"I guess not," Dottie agreed.

Billy Whinner headed for home in the opposite direction, and the kids headed toward Webb Avenue. "All we know about this bike thief is that he wears sunglasses—which he might not always wear—and he has a metal cutter," said Jimmy.

"We don't have much on our other case, either," said Jay. "I hope T.J. sees something today."

A few blocks away on Webb Avenue, T.J. was, indeed, seeing something. The delivery boy had just arrived in the alley. T.J. quickly looked at his watch. It was exactly one-thirty.

Frantically, T.J. moved back and forth between his telescope and a sketch pad propped on the windowsill. He was trying to sketch the delivery boy while he still had him in sight.

The ten other sketches he had strewn out on the bed behind him were all head shots. He'd done them all from memory. But this was his chance to draw from life, and to get details of the bike.

He sketched quickly, stopping to peer into the telescope every few seconds. Finally, the boy dismounted, dumped the pizza box, and walked off up the street.

T.J. knew from experience that he had about five minutes before the delivery boy would reappear in the alley and pick up the bike and pizza again. He used the opportunity to look at the bike and put the finishing touches on his drawing of it. Then he sat back on his bed and compared his latest sketch with the ones on the covers beside him. T.J. was a sharp observer, and his memory was good. They all looked like the same guy.

Then he picked up a sketch he'd done of Ray, based on Dottie and Jay's description. He sure did look like the guy, too. But there was no way it was him. Unlike Cosmic Cop with his molecular divider ring, Ray couldn't have been in two places at once.

T.J. checked back into the telescope. The pizza was still sitting there. It would be in sorry shape by the time it arrived at its destination. It would be cold, and all the cheese would have oozed over to one side.

As T.J. gazed through the telescope lens, he wondered what else could be in that pie besides tomato sauce and cheese. Jewels hidden in the crust? Government secrets spelled out in anchovies? Or maybe little microchips were disguised as pepperoni.

T.J. tensed as the delivery boy came back into view. He strained his eyes. Yes, it was the same guy. Same red hat and jacket, same size and shape, same sunglasses. The delivery boy fished the pizza box out of the garbage and picked up the bike, same as usual.

Suddenly, though, something unusual happened. Somewhere in Dozerville there must have been a fire. (Or, more likely, Mrs. Felix's cat was caught in a tree.) The shrill whine of the volunteer fire alarm filled the air. It was a familiar noise to T.J., but apparently not to the delivery boy. He started at the sound, and the pizza box slipped from his hand and opened on the sidewalk.

In a flash, T.J. turned his lens on the open box. He gasped when he saw what was in it—or rather what *wasn't* in it. The pizza box was completely empty!

C·H·A·P·T·E·R
7

Across town, Jimmy, Jay, Dottie, and Lee were about to be as shocked as T.J. They didn't know it yet, though. As far as they were concerned, they were just going on a routine check of more pizzerias in search of suspects.

"I say we go to the other two LaCosta pizzerias," Jay suggested. "Manny LaCosta said they copy everything he does, even the way his delivery boys dress."

"Right," Dottie agreed. "That means we already know their delivery guys wear red jackets and red hats."

They headed down the block to Famous LaCosta's Best Pizza. It was a pizzeria very much like Original LaCosta's. Across the front door was a big sign that said, "We weren't first—but we're the best!"

The kids went inside to interview the owner, Vinnie LaCosta. He was a tall, thin man with a head of wiry white hair. "That Manny, my cousin, always had cheese where his brains should have been," he told the kids pleasantly. "I come all the way out here to give him a hand, and what does that mozzarella mind do? He accuses me of trying to muscle in on his dough—in every sense of the word. So here I am, stuck out here on the rolling plains with nothing to do. But I sort of liked it here, so I just did what I do best—I opened a pizzeria." He spread his arms wide with pride. "And as you can see, the rest is a living pizza legend."

"That's interesting," said Jay as he snapped a picture of Vinnie. He really did find this history of the LaCosta family feud fascinating. It surprised him that two people could tell the same story so differently. It occurred to him that the LaCosta story might make a good TV series—*Little Pizzerias on the Prairie*.

"Could you tell us something about your delivery boys for our report?" asked Jimmy.

Vinnie shrugged. "What's to tell? They pick up the pizza, and they deliver it."

"Do your delivery boys stay with you long?" Dottie pressed.

"Naw," said Vinnie. "Delivering pizza is just a job you do summers, or until something better comes along. It's hard to get guys who'll work during school hours because it's not a job anyone out of school usually wants. I have a new guy and, between us, he's the worst. Every delivery takes him almost an hour."

The kids looked at one another. Ray had taken a long time, too. "Is he here now?" asked Jimmy.

"No. He's out on one of his endless deliveries," Vinnie said with a sigh.

The kids thanked Vinnie LaCosta and left the

pizzeria. "I guess our next stop is Amazing LaCosta's across the street," said Lee. The four of them crossed the street and entered the pizzeria. A huge banner was strung across the middle of the place proclaiming, "The other two couldn't get it right. Let the Amazing LaCosta amaze you!"

The owner, Carlo LaCosta, was very outgoing and friendly. His fluffy white hair was swept dramatically across his head to cover the wide bald spot. "Vinnie and Manny were at each other's throats," he told them. "Their Grandma Maria begged me to come out here and patch things up between them. So I drive out with only the best intentions. I even bring them a truckload of tomatoes. What do those two ungrateful dough-throwers do? They start pitching tomatoes at me. Me! The amazing Carlo! Well, I figure if those two can open pizzerias, I can do it better." He looked at his pizzeria fondly. "As you can see, I've done a much better job."

The kids couldn't see that. Except for the banner, the place looked exactly like the other two LaCosta's. They nodded politely, anyway.

Jay photographed Carlo, and the Clues Kids asked him about his delivery boys. *His* daytime delivery boy was also out on a run. "And who knows when he'll be back," added Carlo with an expressive wave of his hand. "Sometime around midnight, maybe. He is the slowest delivery boy I've ever had. Maybe he doesn't know how to ride a bike. Maybe he doesn't even *have* a bike. Come to think of it, I've never seen his bike."

"Never seen it?" asked Lee, his ears alert for a clue.

"Why should I? He comes in on foot and he leaves on foot. I assume the bike is out there. Though maybe I'd better ask him when he returns. *If* he ever returns."

The kids thanked Carlo and hurried out of the pizzeria. "Okay," said Jimmy once they were outside. "We have three delivery boys who are all slow and—"

"Look to your right," Dottie interrupted. About one block away, walking toward them, was a delivery boy wearing sunglasses and a red cap and jacket.

Jay squinted. "Is that Ray?" he asked. "It sure looks like him."

Dottie shielded her eyes from the sun and peered down the block. "I think so," she said. "He's heading toward the wrong pizzeria if it *is* him."

"Wait a minute," said Jay, his eyes going wide as he looked across the street. "If that's Ray, then who's *that*?" Across the street stood another boy in a red cap and jacket. He was also wearing sunglasses, and was the same height and build as Ray.

"This is getting very weird," muttered Lee. The other kids followed his gaze down the block to the left. A *third* Ray in red hat, jacket, and sunglasses was walking down the street.

"Let's get out of here," said Dottie. She was beginning to feel as though she were in some science-fiction movie, where everyone was turned into identical pizza deliverers.

"Stay calm," said Jimmy. "They don't know we're on to them. Just pretend we're a bunch of kids hanging out in front of the pizzeria."

"We *are* a bunch of kids hanging out in front of the pizzeria," Jay pointed out.

"You know what I mean," snapped Jimmy. "Act casual, and keep your ears open."

The three delivery boys met in the street, just a few feet away from where the kids were standing. They were all almost exactly the same height and weight. Seeing them together, the kids noticed slight differences—one guy stood with a slouch, another kid kept cracking his knuckles—but they looked remarkably alike.

"I've got to get a shot of this," whispered Jay.

"Careful," Dottie warned. "Remember, these guys could be spies."

Jay nodded, and then crept over to a parked car near where the boys stood in the street. Crouching low, he framed them in the lens of his camera. *Snap*. He got one picture.

"That was a close one today," he heard one of them say. From the voice, he was pretty sure that one was Ray.

"Yeah, you're getting sloppy," the sloucher scolded the knuckle-cracker.

"I'll get it together before the big switch," the knuckle-cracker assured them.

"You'd better," said the sloucher. "It's coming up soon, and we have to be ready."

Snap. Jay took another picture. He was about to sneak away when suddenly the sloucher looked up at him. "What are you staring at, kid?" he demanded harshly.

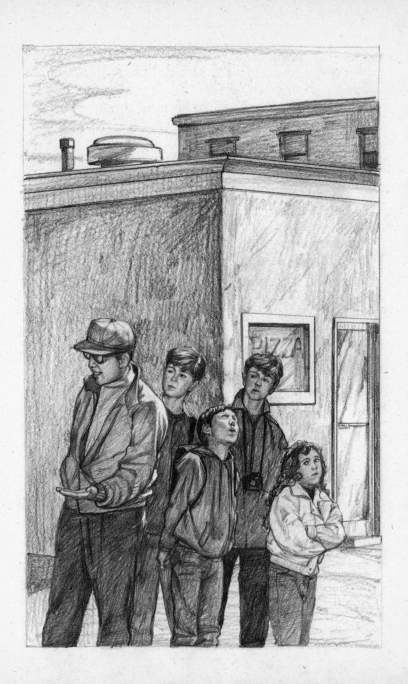

"N . . . n . . . nothing," stammered Jay.

"Is that so?" growled the sloucher, lunging and grabbing Jay by the arm.

"I . . . um . . . no . . . I."

At that moment there was a pitiful wail of a little girl crying. Dottie stepped toward them, her face wet with tears. "You're hurting my brother," she sobbed.

The sloucher let go of Jay's arm. "Hey, don't cry, kid," he said uncomfortably. "Someone might hear you."

Dottie continued to cry at the top of her lungs. The three delivery boys looked up and down the street nervously to see if Dottie's crying had alerted anyone.

"Let's just split," Ray suggested anxiously. "I have to get back to work, anyway." Just as they'd arrived, the three walked off in opposite directions.

"Thanks, Dottie," said Jay. "Those guys are scary. I didn't know you could make yourself cry like that."

Dottie grinned and pulled a compact red plastic water pistol from the back pocket of her jeans. She shut her eyes and squirted herself in the face. "Instant tears," she said proudly. "It was T.J.'s idea."

Jay and Dottie joined Jimmy and Lee. Jay told them what he'd heard about the big switch. "I wonder what that means?" said Jimmy.

"Those guys look like big trouble to me," said Jay. "I think we'd better figure out what they're up to, and fast!"

C·H·A·P·T·E·R
8

*T*he kids looked closely
at the sketches T.J. had done of the delivery
boy. They were all sitting on his bed, having an
emergency meeting to discuss what to do next.

"Let's review the facts," said Jimmy, holding
a sketch in two hands. "We now have three clues.
One, we know that there are two other Ray
look-alikes out there. Two, we know that sometimes they walk, and sometimes they ride bikes.
And three—thanks to T.J.'s totally excellent spy
work—we now have the very weird fact that
the pizza box they're riding around with is
empty. At least, it was empty today."

"And, four, don't forget that there's a big
switch coming up," Jay reminded him.

"What does it all mean?" cried Lee, flopping
down flat on the bed in frustration.

The kids sat quietly and thought hard. There
had to be a connection among all these facts. If
only they could find it.

T.J. thumped his cast against the headboard
of the bed. Benny the handyman hadn't been
able to come fix the stairs. Therefore T.J. hadn't

had the chance to use the heavy clippers the Chief had loaned Benny. He could hold out until Sunday, but after that he'd have to go back to school, and the cast would have to come off, one way or another.

Thinking about this reminded T.J. of something else. "I'm almost better," he told the others. "So we'd better come up with some clues before next Monday. Otherwise I'll be back in school, and I won't be able to spy on the alley anymore."

Jimmy rapped his forehead lightly with his fist. "Think, think, think!" he urged himself.

Suddenly Jay's eyes lit up. He picked up one sketch, then another. "These aren't all the same guy in these sketches," he said quietly. The kids crowded close and looked at the two sketches. "See," he pointed out, "the guy in this sketch had a pointy nose, but the one in this sketch had a rounded nose, like Ray. They look so much alike that I never noticed the slight differences."

"It makes sense," said Jimmy. "These sketches are of the three different guys we saw today."

"That explains why the delivery boy seemed to drop the stuff off and then pick it up himself," said Lee. "He really wasn't. Another look-alike guy was really picking it up."

"All right!" cried Jimmy happily. "Now we're getting somewhere!"

"Yeah! Okay!" the kids cheered.

Then there was silence. "Where exactly are we getting?" asked Lee. "We still don't know what these guys are up to or what's so special about that pizza box. And what's the big switch?"

The kids went back to thinking hard. After some humming and sighing and a lot of squirming, Jimmy finally spoke. "If nobody has any ideas, I say we get down there into that alley and do some more detective work."

"Smudge," said Jay, using Lee's Clues Kids code name, "we need some fingerprints."

"I'll go dust that garbage can," Lee said, and he hopped off the bed to get his fingerprinting set.

"I'll go with you," said Jay, sliding off the bed behind him. "I want to get those pictures I took today developed in the Quick Flash place down the street. Then I'll join you in the alley."

"I'll come, too," offered Dottie. "I don't think Smudge should go down into that alley alone. It's too creepy."

"What help would you be, Short Stuff?" chuckled Jimmy.

Dottie spun around twice and landed a neat karate chop on Jimmy's shinbone. "Ow!" cried Jimmy, rubbing his leg. "Where did you learn to do that?"

"Cosmic did it last week, don't you remember?" Dottie grinned. She put her hands behind her back and rubbed them. She didn't want Jimmy to know that her "neat" karate move had hurt like crazy. "Any more questions, Jaws?" Jimmy didn't answer.

"Hurry up, if you're coming," called Lee from the door.

"T.J., uh, I mean, Smoke Screen and I will keep watch from up here," said Jimmy.

"Hey, lazy, it was your idea to go down there and dig up some clues," said Jay.

Jimmy rubbed his leg. "Yeah, well, I didn't expect to have a bruised shinbone when I said that," he grumbled.

Jay rolled his eyes, then ran to his room and got his camera while Lee collected his fingerprinting equipment. Dottie went to the medicine cabinet and pulled out a roll of gauze. She wrapped it around her hands—just in case she had to use the Cosmic karate chop for real.

In a few minutes they were down in the alley. Everything was quiet. A row of empty cartons, piled high, lined the white cement wall. Suddenly something inside one carton moved. Lee and Jay jumped back. Dottie raised her gauze-wrapped hands, ready to strike.

It moved again. The kids could hear their own hearts pounding. Their imaginations were working overtime. What if one of the delivery boys had seen them coming and was hiding behind the boxes? What if he leaped out and threw them in a box and shipped them off to whatever foreign government he was working for? What if—

Something gray shot out from under the box. Another gray shape followed it. "*Aaaahhhh!*" the kids screamed. They jumped back as two small field mice darted past them and scampered down the alley.

"Oh my gosh! Oh my gosh!" panted Dottie, her hand over her mouth. "I was really scared."

"Me, too," Jay admitted. "The three of us just have to calm down. As far as these guys know, we're just three kids playing in an alley. They won't suspect us."

"You're right," agreed Lee. "I'm just an innocent kid practicing my fingerprinting techniques
by dusting a garbage can for prints."

"Right," said Jay, trying to sound confident.
"I'll be back, but if you finish up before I get
here, just go home. No sense hanging around
here longer than you have to. And if you run
into any trouble, remember, T.J. and Jimmy are
watching from upstairs."

Jay left, and Lee got to work on the empty can.
He tipped it on its side and had Dottie hold it
steady. Then he took a small jar of black powder
and a brush from the pocket of his jacket. Tap-
ping the jar gently, he poured a small amount
onto the can, then spread it with the brush.

"Hey, you're getting better at this," Dottie com-
plimented him. Lee usually wound up with more
of the powder on himself than anywhere else.

Lee then took out his special fingerprinting
tape and started picking up prints. "This thing
is loaded with prints," he said excitedly.

"Of course it is," said Dottie. "The sanitation
workers, the store owners, anybody who comes
along and throws out trash."

Lee wasn't interested in this logic. "You never
know what might turn up," he said knowingly
as he lifted prints onto the tape.

Just then they were startled by a hissing sound.
A black cat raced toward them, followed closely
be a small dog with a leash flapping behind it.
The cat jumped up onto the overturned can and
arched its back at the dog.

Not wanting to be in the middle of a cat-and-

dog fight, Dottie let go of the can. It rolled back on Lee, completely covering his face, hands, and jacket with black powder.

"Thanks a lot!" yelled Lee, brushing himself off.

"Sorry," said Dottie. The little dog yapped at the cat until an old woman rounded the corner of the alley.

"Shame on you, Ignatz," she scolded. The little dog's ears drooped, and he waddled back to his owner with his tail dragging between his stubby legs. In a flash, the cat disappeared down the alley.

Lee held up his empty jar. "I dropped it when the cat surprised me. I'm out of powder, and my prints are ruined."

"Let's go home and get you cleaned up," Dottie suggested, brushing off Lee's jacket.

"This was a waste of time," mumbled Lee gloomily as they left the alley.

There was a line at the Quick Flash photo shop. By the time Jay got out, almost twenty minutes had gone by. He returned to the alley and found it empty. He glanced up at T.J.'s bedroom window and waved. Jay could see the tiny figure of T.J. peeking out from behind the telescope and waving back.

The next thing Jay saw was the overturned garbage can still streaked with Lee's black fingerprint powder. He caught his breath, wondering what could have happened, and ran over to the can. On the one hand, it wasn't unusual for Lee to leave a mess behind. On the other hand, he couldn't figure out why Lee had dusted half the alley. There was powder everywhere.

What if one of the delivery boys had come along and startled Lee and Dottie? Maybe there'd been a fight. He looked up at the window of the Klinks' house. Wouldn't T.J. have noticed if something went wrong?

Just then there was a rumbling in the boxes. Jay jumped, then laughed at himself. *I'm not falling for that again,* he thought. *I can't believe we let two mice scare us out of our wits.*

He continued down the alley, searching for any clues he could find. At first there was nothing, but then he spotted it. Sticking out from under one of the cartons was something brown and furry. Sucking in his breath, he knelt down, grabbed hold of the fur, and pulled.

"Yiiiihhhh!" he cried out. The tail had come off in his hands! In a minute, Jay recovered and looked down at the tail again. It was bushy and golden. A foxtail. As he ran his hand through it, he realized it wasn't even real fur. That's when he remembered. Billy Whinner had had a new foxtail on the back of his stolen bike! He remembered Billy whining about it in the schoolyard.

He was so busy thinking about the foxtail that he barely paid attention to the rumbling in the cartons. He assumed it was more mice. But some sense of danger crept in to alert him that something wasn't right. *That's a lot of noise for a mouse to make,* he thought, just as he looked up and saw the entire stack of cartons come tumbling down on top of him.

C·H·A·P·T·E·R
9

"*T*here he is!" cried Jimmy. Dottie and Lee followed Jimmy to the back of the alley where Jay was climbing out from under a heap of cartons.

"Are you okay?" asked Lee.

"Yeah," said Jay, rubbing his head and sounding a little stunned. "Did you guys see what happened?"

"T.J. was watching and saw the boxes go over," Jimmy told him. "You were too far into the alley for him to see who did it, though. We were all upstairs with him and we ran right down." Jimmy dusted off his brother's back. "Whoever pushed these over on top of you must have come up from the back of the alley and then run down again, because we didn't see anyone come out onto Webb Avenue."

"I don't see anyone either," said Jay. "I was busy looking at this foxtail I found." He pushed away several cartons, trying to find the tail. It wasn't there. He tossed more cartons out of the way. Still no tail.

"I found a foxtail in this alley, just like the

one on Billy Whinner's bike," he told them. "Help me look for it." All four of them dug through the boxes, but they came up empty-handed.

"I bet whoever knocked these boxes over on you took the tail," Jimmy said. "Are you sure it was Billy's?"

"No, I'm not sure," Jay admitted. "But it seems like a pretty big coincidence."

"Maybe whoever stole Billy's bike rode it through this alley," Dottie suggested.

"Boy! If that's true, this alley is like Crime Central," said Lee, looking around anxiously.

"It also means the bike thief saw Jay find the tail," added Jimmy with a shiver. He didn't like the idea of the criminal being that close to Jay.

"We have so many clues, but none of them fit together," Dottie complained as the kids headed out of the alley.

Jimmy checked his watch. "Hey, *Cosmic Cop* is about to start."

The kids turned toward the house. "I want to get a pack of cupcakes," Dottie said, heading for the deli. "I'll meet you back home."

Dottie pulled seventy-five cents from her pants pocket, the last of her two-dollar weekly allowance. She liked to spend it sparingly until Friday, then splurge on something gooey and sweet. Each Saturday she'd get the next week's allowance and start all over again.

She skipped up the front steps of the deli, already tasting the creamy chocolate icing. She reached for the door handle—and stopped short.

Two beady brown eyes were staring down at her from the other side of the glass door. It was Ray!

It was the first time Dottie had seen him without his sunglasses, and she didn't like what she saw. His eyes were cold. They narrowed as he stared at Dottie. His lip turned up into a sneer.

An icy panic seized Dottie, and she ran from the door as quickly as she could. She didn't stop until she had bounded up the Klinks' front steps and into the living room. "It's . . . it's . . . it's him!" she cried. "He's there at the deli!"

The boys were engrossed in Cosmic's escape from Stella Slick's deadly Mud Monster, but they saw how upset Dottie was and turned away from the TV. (And for them to turn away from *Cosmic* . . . well, you know Dottie was really upset!)

"What's the matter?" asked Lee.

"It was Ray. He was in the deli," said Dottie, trying to calm herself.

Jimmy jumped off the recliner. "Did he hurt you?"

"No. He just *looked* at me with these horrible eyes." Dottie narrowed her big green eyes and scrunched up her eyebrows, trying to imitate Ray.

"That would scare anybody," said T.J.

"But it was worse," Dottie said. "His eyes were real mean. It was as if he was trying to threaten me."

"It *is* suspicious that he was near the alley

just when those cartons went over on Jay," said Jimmy.

"Maybe he just stopped for a soda or something," Lee suggested.

"Maybe," Jimmy admitted, "but it's awfully coincidental. He could have dumped the boxes on Jay, and then ducked into the back door of the deli."

"I don't like this," said Dottie, still shaken from the awful look on Ray's face. "I think we should tell the Chief."

"Tell me what?" asked the Chief, who had come to the door just in time to hear Dottie's last comment. The kids looked at one another. Without speaking, they knew the time had come to let the Chief in on what was happening. It was all getting a little too scary to handle on their own.

As usual, Jimmy did the talking. He explained about the delivery boy T.J. had seen, and how he'd turned out to be three delivery boys in identical hats and jackets—who were probably really spies. He told him about the empty pizza box, and how someone had knocked a pile of cartons over on Jay.

"And now this guy Ray just gave me the goofy eyeball," Dottie chimed in.

"The what?" asked the Chief, sounding amused.

Dottie narrowed her eyes again in her version of the way Ray had scowled at her. The Chief chuckled softly. "Oh, *that* goofy eyeball," he said. He sat down in his big comfortable chair and looked at the kids seriously. "Now, listen.

What do you think a band of international spies would be doing here in Dozerville?"

The kids glanced at one another, then shrugged their shoulders.

"Right," said the Chief. "Other than smuggling out pizza recipes, there isn't too much spies would want in Dozerville."

"But how do you explain the empty pizza box? And what's going on out in the alley?" T.J. challenged.

It was the Chief's turn to shrug his broad shoulders. "Who knows? I bet that all you've stumbled onto is a bunch of delivery boys who've discovered a way to goof off and still get paid."

"What about the missing foxtail, and the boxes someone dumped on Jay?" asked Jimmy.

"The tail could have come from anywhere, and Jay probably knocked down the boxes when he pulled the tail out from under them," the Chief answered. "It's probably still sitting under a box."

"What about the goofy eyeball?" asked Dottie.

The Chief laughed and ruffled Dottie's hair. "I'd say, little miss, that the goofy eyeball is something you do very well, and that this Ray character just happened to run into a little girl with a very active imagination."

Pulling himself up from his chair, the Chief headed out of the living room. "Now forget this silliness," he told them. He headed into the hallway, and then turned back. "And T.J., I want you out of that crazy cast."

"I'm waiting for Benny to return your clippers," T.J. replied. "I thought he was coming today."

"I thought so, too," said the Chief. "But he never showed. If he doesn't come by tomorrow, I'm fixing those stairs myself."

They went back to the TV set and *Cosmic Cop*. They hadn't seen how it happened, but Cosmic now had the Mud Monster in a hammerlock at his side. "You may have thought I was beaten, but you should know I never give up!" Cosmic said bravely. "That's my motto: Never give up! It's not original, but it sounds good!"

Jay snapped off the TV. His jaw was set into a stubborn expression they'd all seen before. "We're not giving up, either!" he told them. "The Clues Kids have just begun to fight!"

C·H·A·P·T·E·R
10

*I*t was Saturday morning. The first stop on the kids' crusade to unravel the mystery was a trip to the *Dozerville Herald*. Why? you may ask. Because the kids had an informant at the *Herald*—ace reporter Tabby Lloyd.

They entered the quiet press room and spotted Tabby sitting at her messy desk. Even though it was the weekend, they knew they'd find her there. Tabby was a go-getter. She worked all the time.

Tabby was only twenty-two, but she was determined to be the best reporter on the paper. Because she was so young, her bosses always gave her assignments like covering the construction of the twenty-seventh pizza parlor in town, or reporting on the Cat Queen contest. Now and then she got to do a good story. But Tabby hungered to do even more solid reporting, crack crimes, and expose evil—not crown cats.

She looked up and sighed when she saw the kids coming toward her. She liked them well enough, but in the past some of their "tips" had gotten her into trouble. Like the time she brought the police and a photographer down to expose a doll theft ring and it turned out to be a new charitable organization collecting toys for the less fortunate. Jimmy had given her that "tip." She considered it the single most embarrassing moment in her entire twenty-two years.

Tabby considered diving under her desk, but decided against it. It was too late. She knew the kids had spotted her. There was clearly nothing else to do but smile and listen to what they had to say. She had to admit that every once in a while they actually stumbled onto something.

"How are my pals?" she welcomed them, tossing back her long, dark, frizzy hair. "What can I do for you?"

"Hi, Miss Lloyd," said Jimmy. "I may have a really gigantic story for you this time."

"How nice," Tabby said with a note of insincerity. "Let's have it."

Jimmy told her all about the case they'd been working on. When he was done, Tabby shook her head. "Can't use it," she said.

"But we need you to," Jimmy pleaded. "If you write a story about it, then the spies might get nervous and make a mistake. We want to find a way to upset them."

"If I wrote that story, the only one who would be upset is my boss. Spies? In Dozerville? Give me a break."

"I *am* giving you a break," Jimmy persisted. "This story could make your career."

"Make it go away, you mean." Tabby laughed softly. "Sorry, it's too far out."

Lee stepped forward. "I have another story you might be able to write about," he offered. He told her all about the rash of bike thefts in town, and about how his own bike had been nabbed.

"And Lee almost caught the guy," Jay added. "He chased him when he was stealing our friend Billy's bike."

Tabby tapped the end of her pencil on the desk decisively. "Now, that's a story I can use," she said. She took down all the information the kids could give her on the bike thefts.

"I have a question, Miss Lloyd," Dottie spoke up. "What do bike thieves do with all the bikes? They can't ride them all. And if they tried to sell them in town, people would recognize their own bikes."

Tabby leaned back in her chair. "Have you ever heard of a fence?" she asked.

"Sure we have," Dottie answered.

"We have a fence in our backyard," said Jay, teasing.

Tabby didn't smile. "So you know that a fence is someone who buys stolen goods. The fence pays the thief, then takes the stuff to another town where people won't recognize it and sells it there. He sells it for more money than he paid the thief. The thief is usually willing to take less just to get rid of the stuff."

"I'm curious," said Lee. "Why do they call him a fence?"

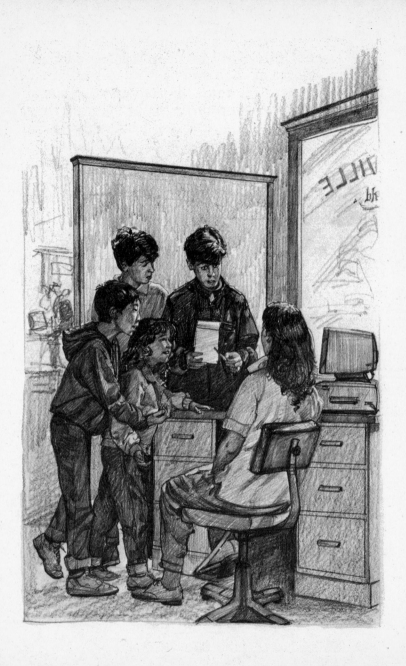

"I'm not sure, but I bet it comes from a time when thieves stole things and just passed them over the fence to someone on the other side. That way, if they were caught, they wouldn't have any stolen goods on them and they could claim innocence."

"That's real interesting," said Jimmy, "but it doesn't help with our pizza delivery case."

"Sorry, kiddo," said Tabby. "If you hear any more about the bike thieves, let me know. That's the biggest news in Dozerville in a while. Thanks for the scoop."

The kids thanked Tabby for her time and left the press room. Their next stop was the Quick Flash photo store to pick up Jay's pictures. "Let's check in with T.J. and go over these pictures at home," Jimmy suggested.

When they got home they found T.J. wrapped in white bed sheets and wearing a turban made of old rags. The cast was still on his leg.

"That costume will blend in just great here in Dozerville," said Jay sarcastically. "No one will notice you at all."

"This disguise isn't for Dozerville," T.J. answered confidently. "I'm planning ahead in case we have to follow these spies to the airport. This is my international traveler disguise. I needed something that would cover my cast."

"Take that dumb thing off, already!" cried Dottie who was tired of hearing the *clump*, *clump*, *clump* of T.J. walking around on his cast.

T.J. looked at his leg and sighed. "I worked so hard on this, I hate to ruin it."

Jay spread his photos out on T.J.'s bed. The kids laughed when they saw the shot of Manny LaCosta with pizza dough coming down on his face. They grew serious as they studied the menacing faces of the three look-alike delivery boys that Jay had take outside Amazing LaCosta's. "What creeps," Dottie muttered.

Jay picked up the photo he'd taken the day before. "I took these when Billy Whinner's bike was stolen," he said. "Darn! The thief's head got cut out of the shot."

T.J. took the photo from Jay and studied it quietly, as the others pored over the remaining pictures. Without a word, he picked up one of his sketches from the dresser at the side of his bed. It was the one he'd done of the delivery boy on the bike. He held it side by side with the photo.

Jimmy noticed T.J.'s serious concentration and looked over his shoulder. "That's the same bike!" he cried. "It has the same high handlebars and banana seat. When did you do that sketch?"

"Friday," T.J. answered. "It was around one-thirty. I remember because it occurred to me that the delivery guy was early."

"Friday is when Billy's bike was stolen!" said Lee. "And it was just after one o'clock. I'm sure of that, because school had just let out."

"But how did the delivery boy get Billy's bike?" asked Jay.

There was silence for a moment, and then it hit them. "Unless the bike thief *was* one of the delivery boys without his jacket and hat!" Jimmy spoke the words they were all thinking.

"That means those guys aren't spies at all!" cried Dottie. "They're bike thieves!"

"I'll bet that's what they're doing in the alley," said Jimmy. "They steal a bike, then they put on their pizza delivery outfits to disguise themselves. They drop the bike off, and then another delivery boy picks it up and rides off with it."

"That would also explain why they take so long on deliveries," added Jay. "Remember? All the owners were complaining. They must have gotten hold of an empty pizza box just to make themselves look innocent as they rode around on stolen bikes."

"And the big switch!" Dottie exclaimed. "I know what it is now! The fence! The fence is coming to switch the bikes for money. That's got to be it!"

"How dumb could we be?" said Jimmy. "All this time we thought we had two cases, and they were really the same case."

Lee headed for the door. "We have to go tell the Chief. If we don't catch these guys before the big switch, then all the bikes will be gone and we won't have any evidence. And I'll never see my bike again."

Jimmy and Jay started for the door. "The Klinks aren't home," Dottie told them. She pulled a note out of her pants pocket. "You guys passed right by this note when you rushed in here. It says they've gone to a town meeting about widening Webb Avenue."

"That means they're down at the town hall,"

said Jay. "Come on, let's go down and meet them. This can't wait."

"I'm coming, too," said T.J., pulling the rags from his head. "I feel fine, and I'm tired of being cooped up around here."

"You'd better not," said Jimmy. "The Klinks would be mad. Besides, we don't have time to wait for you to hop along on that stupid cast."

T.J. plopped back down on his bed. "No fair," he muttered as the others rushed out the door. He went to the window and watched as the kids hurried up the street. He looked at them until they were just small dots. He was about to turn away when a movement in the alley caught his eye. Quickly looking into the telescope, T.J. saw a delivery boy dressed in red step out of the alley. Then he saw the delivery boy lift a pair of binoculars to his eyes and stare right back up at him.

T.J. gasped and jumped away from the window. The delivery boy was on to him. He knew T.J. had been spying on him, and he knew where he lived. Barely breathing, T.J. crept to the side of the window and peeked out again.

The delivery boy had been joined by two others, also in red jackets and hats. They looked up at the window and folded their arms across their chests. Without taking their eyes off the window, they began to cross Webb Avenue. They were heading straight for the Klinks' house. Instinctively, T.J. knew the horrible truth. They were coming to get him.

C·H·A·P·T·E·R
11

T.J. thought he had been scared before. He now knew he had been wrong. What he'd experienced in the past was mere nervousness compared to the heart-pounding, mind-numbing, goose-bumping terror he now felt. These creeps were after him, and he was all alone. They'd probably been watching the house and knew there was no one there to help him.

Moving as fast as he could, T.J. hopped into the Klinks' bedroom. He grabbed the phone on their night table. He punched in the number of the Dozerville police department. Then he waited. The phone rang . . . and rang . . . and rang. "Come on, pick up, pick up," said T.J.

Finally there was a voice on the other end. "Hello."

It sounded like Sergeant Beasley. "Hello, this is T.J. Booker," T.J. said quickly. "I need help. I'm at—"

There was a click, and then silence. The phone was dead. Maybe they cut the line in the backyard, T.J. thought.

T.J. thumped down the stairs. He headed for the front door, but stopped short. The brass doorknob was being jiggled by someone on the other side.

He turned and hopped through the dining room toward the back door in the kitchen. He stopped in the doorway and listened. Someone was pulling at the wooden frame of the screen door. There was a snap, and then a loud creak as the door gave way. T.J. heard the sound of metal scratching on metal. The thieves were picking the lock of the inside back door. Apparently, they knew what they were doing, because in seconds, T.J. heard the bolt sliding out of the locked position. As soon as they got through the flimsy latch above it, they would be in.

"Think fast! Think fast!" T.J. whispered to himself desperately. He hopped out of the dining room. *Darn this stupid cast,* he thought. Things were bad enough without being slowed down with this thing. If only Benny had come when he was supposed to!

Benny! An idea came to T.J. He grabbed a wooden chair from the dining room and hobbled to the cellar door. He set it down in the hall and quietly opened the door. Sliding down onto the floor, he leaned down and picked up the loose third step and put it down next to him on the floor. Stretching down farther, he tried to get the top of the fourth step up.

He couldn't reach it.

He tried again and managed to lift it with the

90

tips of his fingers. He poked again, and it clattered down the stairs.

A sound in the kitchen made T.J. flinch. They were inside! Pulling himself to his feet, he lifted the chair and heaved it down the cellar steps with all his might. Just as quickly, he ducked into the coat closet just off the hall.

His heart was pounding so loudly it filled his head. It seemed that the thieves would surely be able to hear it and find him. As he clutched Mrs. Klink's fake-fur coat to help stop his trembling, he heard heavy footsteps come into the hallway.

"The noise came from here," said one.

The other one laughed in a low, nasty way. "Cellar door's open. We've got the little rat cornered. Let's get him and teach him a lesson he won't forget."

T.J. heard the cellar door open and held his breath. For a minute there was silence, then . . .
Thump! Bang! Crash!

"One," T.J. counted.

Thud-thud-thud-thud . . . bang!

"Two," whispered T.J.

"What the heck's going on down—Hey!" *Bang! Bang! Bang! Thump!*

"Three!" cried T.J. as he flung open the closet door. He took two hops and threw himself against the cellar door, slamming it shut. *Click-clack.* He turned the lock in the door.

"Hey!"

"What the—"

"Let us out of here!"

Panting heavily, T.J. leaned against the cellar door. Suddenly there was more jangling at the front door. "Oh, no!" T.J. cried. "There are more of them!"

The door was opening. He lunged for it, throwing all his weight against it. It was no use. Whoever was on the other side was too strong!

The next thing T.J. saw was better than a new baseball glove, better than a banana split ... better than Christmas! It was the Chief's face staring down at him. "It's just me, son," he said. "What's going on?"

The Chief came in, followed by Mrs. Klink and the rest of the kids. "They're in there," T.J. gasped, pointing at the cellar door. "I have the ... the ... the thieves. Locked in. They were coming to get me."

The Chief stared at the door for a second, and then understood what had happened. His face turned red, beginning at his neck and traveling up to his snowy white hairline. He was mad. Real mad. "They broke into our house!" he growled.

Mrs. Klink grabbed his arm as he marched toward the door. "There are three of them and one of you. Just let the police handle this."

Dottie, Jimmy, Jay, and Lee clustered around the Chief and Mrs. Klink. "I'll call them," Dottie volunteered.

T.J. grabbed her arm. "They cut the phone lines," he said.

"They what!" Phil Klink roared.

"I'll go next door," Dottie said quickly. And off she ran.

The others scurried after the Chief as he headed into the kitchen. He filled a very large kettle full of ice-cold water, and threw in two trays of ice cubes just for good measure. Then he walked back to the cellar door and unlocked it.

The three thieves stood on the stairs just below the hole where the third and fourth steps had been. "Let us out of here!" the one with the slouch cried.

"You'll be sorry," Ray threatened.

"Yeah," agreed the third, cracking his knuckles angrily.

With this the Chief lifted the pot and doused them with freezing water. Then he shut the door and relocked it. "Sorry, dear," he said, turning to Mrs. Klink. "I had to do something. It makes my blood boil that they would have the nerve to come right in here and threaten one of my kids." He pulled T.J. to his side and squeezed him tight. "You're a brave boy, T.J.," he said. "And darned clever, too."

T.J. smiled and hugged back. Hard. It was a good feeling to go from being a dead duck to being an alive and happy master of disguise.

In the next second, the air filled with the sound of wailing police sirens. Three squad cars pulled into the driveway, and six members of the Dozerville police force bounded up the Klinks' front steps.

"What's the problem here?" asked Sergeant Beasley.

"No problem," Jimmy told him. "We have

the bike thieves you've been looking for all locked up—and cooled down—in our cellar."

The next person to rush in the door was Tabby Lloyd. "I was researching the bike theft case at the police department when the call came in," she said. Behind her was a photographer from the newspaper who said nothing, but kept snapping pictures.

The police opened the cellar door. T.J. handed them one of the missing steps, which they replaced. Then they marched the thieves out.

Sergeant Beasley stepped up to Ray and pulled off his sunglasses. "Ray Wheatley," he said. "I should have known you'd come back." He turned to the Klinks and the kids. "My son went to school with these three. They're brothers. They were the worst kids in Wrighter Elementary. The principal celebrated for three days when they moved away. Now they'll be going away again—to jail."

The three thieves just glared at the kids as the police took them away in handcuffs. "What about my bike?" Lee asked Sergeant Beasley.

"These three all live together in a rented house. I'll send a car over there right now. I'm sure we'll have your bike back to you within the hour," he answered.

Lee smiled, and he wasn't alone. All the kids were smiling. "Okay," said Tabby Lloyd. "Get together for a picture." The kids gathered around the Klinks.

The photographer snapped the shot. "You can expect to see that on the front page of the *Herald*

———•———

tomorrow," Tabby told them happily. She interviewed T.J. about what had happened to him after Jimmy told her how the thieves had operated. "Now this is news!" she said, writing frantically on her pad.

Tabby rushed out the door. "Stop the presses!" she yelled into the air as she scurried to her car.

"That's another case solved," said Jimmy, rubbing his hands together briskly.

"We did it again!" chirped Dottie.

"Hooray for us!" yelled Jay.

"Hip-hip-hooray!" Lee and T.J. cried out together.

Just then, there was a rap on the open front door. It was Benny the handyman. "Hi," he said, "I'm here to fix those steps. Sorry it took so long."

The Chief ushered him in. "Your timing was perfect, Benny. Simply perfect," he said.

The Clues Kids were too excited to sit still. There was nothing more satisfying than solving a crime. Nothing except perhaps a round of super banana splits over at Maltese's and Falcone's Ice Cream Parlor. And that's exactly what the Chief and Mrs. Klink treated them to—after Benny cut the cast off T.J.'s leg.

That night, the kids in Dozerville went to sleep knowing that their bikes would still be there in the morning, and snored just a little louder, thanks to five fearless, ever-watchful, always nosy children known as the Clues Kids.